THE CHRISTMAS EVE GHOST

For Alice

First published 2010 by Walker Books Ltd
87 Vauxhall Walk, London SE11 5HJ

2 4 6 8 10 9 7 5 3 1

This book has been typeset in Mrs Eaves

Printed in China

British Library Cataloguing in Publication Data:
a catalogue record for this book is
available from the British Library

ISBN 978-1-4063-2063-3

www.walker.co.uk

THE CHRISTMAS EVE GHOST

Shirley Hughes

WALKER BOOKS
AND SUBSIDIARIES
LONDON · BOSTON · SYDNEY · AUCKLAND

Once, in the old seaport city of Liverpool, when tramcars clanged up and down the main streets on iron tracks, there lived two children called Bronwen and Dylan.

They had not lived there very long. Mam had brought them there from their village in Wales after their Da had died.

Da had been killed in a mining accident when he was working deep underground. Bronwen could just remember his strong arms and his smell of coal dust. But Dylan was too little to remember him at all.

Mam earned a living for the three of them by doing other people's washing. There were no washing machines in those days and it was very hard work.

She did not have enough money to pay someone to look after Bronwen and Dylan, so, early in the morning before it was light, she had to leave them while they were still asleep.

She pushed the big old pram uphill to the better part of the city where the well-off people lived, to collect their dirty washing.

Mam hurried from house to house, delivering the clean washing and piling up the pram with dirty sheets and towels and shirts and pillowcases.

Then she ran back as fast as she could, worrying and fretting all the way because she hated having to leave the children all alone in the house.

But somehow she always managed to get back before they woke up, in time to make their breakfast porridge.

As soon as she had washed up the breakfast things, Mam set to work.

At the back of the house was a narrow room with a stone floor, called a wash house. In it were a sink, a wash tub and a big iron mangle for wringing out the wet washing.

In the corner was a little brick fire-place with an iron door, and above it was a metal basin with a wooden lid. This was called a "copper".

Bronwen and Dylan watched as Mam lit the fire with sticks and newspaper and put bits of coal on top. Then she filled the basin with cold water from the sink tap and put the lid on.

When the water was hot, Mam pushed the sheets and towels into the basin with soap flakes and began to boil them clean.

Then she stood bent over her wash tub, rubbing and scrubbing at the smaller things with a bar of yellow soap, while the wash house filled up with steam.

When all the things were properly clean she rinsed them in the sink.

After that she wrung them through the big iron mangle.

Sometimes Bronwen and Dylan helped to turn the big wheel, which worked the rollers that squeezed the water out of the washing.

It made them feel very big and strong, turning and turning that wheel for Mam. You had to be careful not to pinch your fingers in the rollers as the washing went through.

The grey sudsy water drained into a big tub underneath. When that was done Mam emptied the tub in the back yard.

If the weather was fine she carried all the washing outside in big baskets and pegged it out on the clothes line to dry.

But if it rained she dried it in the kitchen, draped over wooden frames called "clothes horses" or raised up to the ceiling on a pulley. On those days Bronwen and Dylan ate their dinner among the wet sheets.

Next came the ironing. There was no electricity in their house, so Mam heated up her flat iron over the kitchen stove. She had to take great care not to make it too hot in case it scorched the linen. That would have been a great disaster.

When it was all finished and aired, she folded it beautifully and piled it neatly in the old pram, ready to push it back up the hill early the next morning.

Mam was a big sturdy woman but
she did get very tired and she hated
the city dirt.

In the evenings she was mostly too
tired to do anything but sit in her chair
and look into the fire, remembering
the green valley where she had lived as
a child, and wishing that they were all
back there again.

Sometimes she told Bronwen and
Dylan thrilling stories about dragons
and hauntings, and wicked devils with
tails, and ghosties which came down
the chimney at night.

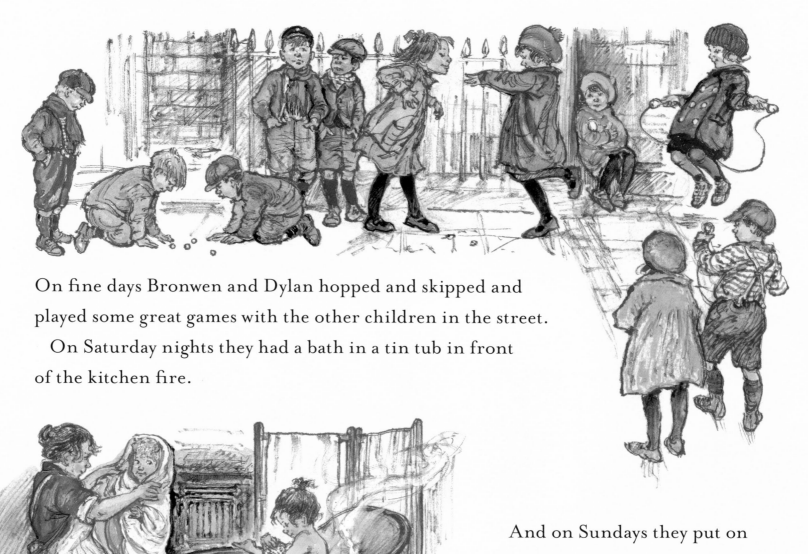

On fine days Bronwen and Dylan hopped and skipped and played some great games with the other children in the street.

On Saturday nights they had a bath in a tin tub in front of the kitchen fire.

And on Sundays they put on their best clothes and went with Mam to sing hymns in Chapel.

In the house next to theirs lived
Mr and Mrs O'Riley and their two
handsome sons.

Mr O'Riley worked at the docks,
unloading great bales of goods from
the holds of ships which had come
into the port from all over the world.

The O'Riley lads worked there too,
alongside their dad. They set out
with all the other men, tramp, tramp,
tramping along the cobbled street.

In the bad times there was no work
for them and no money either, and
they had to stand idle on the street
corner, whiling away the day as
best they could.

Mam never spoke to the O'Rileys except to say "Good morning".

"We keep ourselves to ourselves," she told Bronwen and Dylan. And that meant that they were not to speak to the O'Rileys either.

Bronwen thought it was very strange. There was nothing wrong with the O'Rileys as far as she could see.

But, of course, she did as Mam told her.

The O'Rileys did not go to Chapel. They went to another church.
Once Bronwen had peeped in there and seen beautiful statues and coloured
glass and candles all alight.

She thought it looked lovely, much prettier than their plain chapel with its
whitewashed walls. But when she asked Mam if they could go there one Sunday,
just for a change, Mam's face became very stern and serious. She told Bronwen
that the church was for a different sort of people, not their kind, and that she
was never to look in there again.

Christmas was coming but times were bad and there was no money
to spare. Mam was working long hours to save a bit extra to buy
something nice for Bronwen and Dylan.

At last, on Christmas Eve, all the extra washing was finished and folded
into the pram. Bronwen and Dylan went with Mam, delivering it all
around the houses.

On the way home they saw the brightly-lit shops with dead rabbits and
turkeys and joints of meat hanging up, and people selling toys in the street,
and piles of apples on market barrows.

Bronwen's and Dylan's legs were tired because they had walked so far,
so Mam took them home.

But she still had some more shopping to do. She did not like to leave the children alone in the house after dark, but this evening she took up her purse and told them that she was just going to run down to the shop at the end of the street and that they were to play together like good children until she came back.

"I won't be long," she said. "Don't answer the door if anyone knocks."

After Mam had gone Bronwen settled down to putting her dolls to bed and Dylan watched. She pretended that they were being naughty and not going to sleep until Father Christmas had been.

Dylan said, "I don't think Father Christmas will come to our house anyway, because if he came down our chimney he'd burn his feet!"

"Perhaps he'll come through the back door," said Bronwen.

And then there came a knock.
It was not the front door knocker.
It was coming from the back
of the house.
And it was more like a plonk
than a knock.

"*Plonk!*" it went.

Then

"*Plonk!*

Plonk!"

They both sat still and listened.
It came again:

"*Plonk!*
Plonk!
Plonk!
Plonk!"

Bronwen got up and crept into the back kitchen. Dylan followed, hanging on to her pinafore.

The noise was coming from the wash house. It sounded strange and echoing. Bronwen pushed open the door.

There was only a little pale moonlight coming in from the window by the sink.

"Maybe Father Christmas is coming down the wash-house chimney," said Bronwen.

"Don't go in there, Bron. Please don't!" whispered Dylan.

The noise came again, suddenly. It was certainly coming from the dark corner by the copper.

"Plonk! ... Plonk! ... Plonk!"

"Somebody's hiding in the copper," said Bronwen.

"And that somebody's trying to get out! It's not Father Christmas!
It's that horrid ghostie coming down the chimney to get us!" shrieked Dylan.

And he bolted, screaming, through the kitchen, down the hallway
and out into the street.

Bronwen ran after him. She was screaming too.

They did not run far. They fell straight into the arms of Mrs O'Riley
who was coming home with the family shopping.

"Glory be! What in the world is all this, then?" she cried,
dumping down her baskets.

After she had calmed Bronwen and
Dylan enough to hear their story,
she left her shopping, took them each
by the hand and they all marched
bravely back into the house. When
Mrs O'Riley came with them to the
dark wash house it did not seem nearly
so frightening. Soon the sound came
from behind the copper again:

"*Plonk! … Plonk! … Plonk!*"

"Sure I know what that noise is," said
Mrs O'Riley firmly. "And it's nothing
to be afraid of. You'd better come
along back to my house until your
Ma gets back and then you can see for
yourselves."

But first she said that Bronwen must
leave a note for Mam in case she was
worried about where they had got to.

So Bronwen found a piece of paper
and a stub of pencil and wrote:

Deer Mam
We are gon next dor
lov and ×××
       Bronwen

They propped it up on the
mantelshelf beside the clock.

Mrs O'Riley's house was very different
from theirs. In the hallway was a picture
of Mary and Baby Jesus with a vase of
flowers in front of it. And in the kitchen
there were shelves with shining china
and brass and a delicious smell of stew.

At the back of the house was a wash house just like theirs but turned the other way around and brightly lit. In it were the two O'Riley boys and their dad. They had rigged up a dart board next to the copper and were in the middle of a game.

When they threw a dart it landed on the board – plonk!

"That's the noise you were hearing!" Mrs O'Riley told Bronwen and Dylan kindly. "Sure, and it's nothing but a game of darts! Nothing to be scared of now, is it?"

Bronwen and Dylan stared like two solemn little owls. The O'Riley boys stopped their game and grinned at them.

Mam was very flustered and anxious when she came to fetch them. But she found Bronwen and Dylan sitting happily by the O'Rileys' kitchen fire, eating slices of bread dripping with golden syrup.

"I'm very grateful to you," said Mam to Mrs O'Riley when she heard all about what had happened. "I blame myself for leaving the children alone, but it's so difficult sometimes…"

"Think nothing of it, Mrs Williams," said Mrs O'Riley. "I'll be glad to keep an eye on them any time you need to slip out."

Then Mam and Mrs O'Riley
drank a cup of tea together and
chatted. When it was time to say
goodnight they all wished each
other a happy Christmas.

That night, when Bronwen and Dylan had hung up their stockings and were safely tucked up in bed, Mam told them to remember Da in their prayers and give thanks for all blessings that Christmas night.

"Can I give thanks for Mrs O'Riley and Mr O'Riley and the O'Riley boys too?" asked Dylan.

"Mrs O'Riley was a big blessing to us when we thought there was a horrid ghostie in the wash house," added Bronwen.

Mam did not answer for a moment. Her face was very serious and thoughtful. Then she smiled, and it was like the sun coming out over green fields.

"Yes, of course you must," she said.

A NOTE FROM SHIRLEY HUGHES

I always knew that one day I would make a picture book that drew on my vivid childhood memories of Liverpool in the 1930s. The bustling shops, tramcars and thrilling monumental buildings stood in stark contrast with the cramped squalor of back streets where the struggle to keep clean and make a decent life for a family was very hard.

I found all the domestic details easy to recall. The huge challenge of Monday-morning washday, with the washing all done by hand, the wash tubs, scrubbing boards, mangles and clothes lines which I well remember, are now for most people mercifully a thing of the past. But the kindness of neighbours, like Mrs O'Riley who comes to the rescue when Bronwen and Dylan are sure that a ghost is stalking their wash house, is something we all need and depend upon today as much as ever.

Shirley Hughes